Judy
Slaughter

THE

STEALING OF A

HEALING

THE

STEALING OF A

HEALING

"How to Stay Forever Healed"

Evangelist Mark Dunfee

Dedication

If you have ever been sick and suffered, I dedicate this book to you. The Lord Jesus gave this book to me so that you can walk upon the earth healed until Jesus comes back. This book is dedicated to all who desire to live a long life with fullness of joy until they are satisfied.

With long life will I satisfy him and show him My salvation. (Psalm 91:16 AMPC)

Contents

Introduction

When healing comes, invite it to stay and never let it go. Never lose your faith, and always speak health and healing over your body and family. This book will show you how to get healed and how to stay healed. Learn how to slam the door in the devil's face and keep walking in health and strength. The healing Gospel is true, and to receive your healing and keep it, all you have to do is believe. Jesus gave it to me and now I freely give it to you.

"What do you mean, 'If I can'?" Jesus asked. "Anything is possible if a person believes." (Mark 9:23 NLT)

1

The Stealing of the Word

The thief comes only in order to steal and kill and destroy. I came that they may have and enjoy life, and have it in abundance (to the full, till it overflows). (John 10:10 AMPC)

When God gives you something, the devil will try to steal it. Every time. But you can keep it every time. We are not power-less and we are not victims. We are the healed people of faith.

The little devil is an immediate Word stealer, and in the Good News of the Gospel of Mark, chapter 4:15, we are taught about it:

> And these are they by the way side, where the word is sown; but when they have heard, Satan cometh immediately, and taketh away the word that was sown in their hearts.

If you allow it, the enemy will steal the Word from your heart. This is the Word that, when meditated upon, causes faith to come. It also keeps the faith that you have strong and growing.

If you allow the enemy to get you to meditate on the lies and discouraging thoughts he introduces into your thought life, your faith will weaken. Then sickness will come. And so will lack and poverty, weakness, and even death.

Shutting the Door

Castles in medieval Europe had high walls and strong gates built of mighty and strong stones to keep the enemy out. Watchmen walked on the walls day and night, and they were always alert and positioned for an attack of the enemy. So it is with people of faith who refuse to allow the devil to slip in through the back door and steal any of the blessings of God.

Be well balanced (temperate, sober of mind), be vigilant and cautious at all times; for that enemy of yours, the devil, roams around like a lion roaring [in fierce hunger], seeking someone to seize upon and devour. (1 Peter 5:8 AMPC)

Healing is meant to last for a lifetime. But the devil's satanic ministry is to steal anything that we let him steal. God wouldn't heal someone and then change His mind, or decide to give someone a touch that just lasts for a little while. In the New Living Translation, Romans 11:29 says:

For God's gifts and his call can never be withdrawn.

Open a door and the devil will come right in. Slam the door on wrong thinking, on doubt, and on unbelief, and the enemy will be extremely limited in your life and family. Oh, I have such good news for you and I share it with great joy: Resist the devil and he will flee from you! You don't have to leave any door open for the enemy in your mind.

The Door of Relationships

You may have to close the door to a lot of people who have been speaking words of doubt and unbelief into your spirit. Some of the nicest but most unbelieving people go to church every Sunday. Listen to them and you will get sick and stay sick. Listen to them and you will be poor and stay poor, and all the while they will simply blame it on God.

When you get a revelation of the goodness of God—of how much God loves you, wants to bless you, and wants to heal you and your family—you will never be the same. The thoughts we think, entertain, and meditate on, and the words that we speak, make all the difference. They will either bring blessing or pain into our lives—again and again, and over and over.

What mindsets are you passing down to your family? I do not believe that Christians who are blood-washed can be cursed. But mindsets can be passed down from generations that allow an entrance to pain and misery.

The mindset that you pass onto your children is one that will bring them into prosperity or one that will cause them to live like they were cursed if it were possible. That is why we need to teach our children the Word of God when they are young. I thank God for every Sunday School teacher I had. They used a wooden stand with a flannel--covered board and stuck up paper pictures of Bible characters. They made the Bible come alive to me, and they helped change my life.

The Door of Fear

Don't ever listen to the enemy. Fear, doubt, and unbelief are descendants of the devil. Anytime they come, it is to rob and steal everything God has ever done for you. But the Word of God—especially a verse or a Word that has been specifically made alive to you—when spoken by you, will make the enemy run like you fired a 12-gauge spiritual shotgun at him.

Take that Word that the Holy Spirit has quickened and made alive to you, and meditate on it over and over again. It will strengthen you every time and stop the devil in his tracks, keeping him from being allowed to steal your healing.

You don't ever have to fear. Never forget that through the Word you can put a stop to the devil's evil work of stealing anything he can.

Fear is the opposite of faith. Fear opens a door for the enemy. *Lock your mind from the enemy by only meditating on God's Word, and never the enemy's lies.*

It is amazing the people who lock their doors every night yet never close their minds to the lies of the enemy. Here's how you can tell it is the enemy: There will be doubt, confusion, no peace, and no joy. All of these are signs of the wicked one. You don't have to yield to that any more than you have to open your front door during the winter and let the icy wind blow in; or any more than you have to open your window during the rain and let the wind blow rain inside.

Always replace a bad thought from the enemy with a *good thought* of *God's truth* from a Scripture verse.

> Finally, brethren, whatsoever things are true, whatsoever things are honest, whatsoever things are just, whatsoever things are pure, whatsoever things are lovely, whatsoever things are of good report; if there be any virtue, and if there be any praise, think on these things. (Philippians 4:8)

2

The Door of Thoughts and Words

When Jesus begins the work of completely setting someone free, so many times the enemy comes in the form of a thought. Demonic suggestions and lies are placed in a person's mind about their particular situation. *Then the enemy tries to get a person to speak words of doubt and fear.*

Always remember, God will never do anything bad to you. He is always trying to bring healing and something good into your life. *But you have to give God some faith words to work with.*

The worst thing that you can do in a time of testing is to allow unbelief to arise in your heart. You can open a door for the enemy just by speaking thoughts that come into your mind that do not line up with the Word. It causes sickness and difficulties to return with aches and pains.

Oh, the times I have seen people confess how things are, how they feel, and how they have to learn everything the hard way. Words of doubt and unbelief can only cause things to get worse. Always be motivated by faith and never be motivated by fear.

When people ask unbelieving-believer

friends about their situation, they rarely get a good report. Instead, they are told tales of pain and suffering and what happened to a person's great-uncle.

So many people study lying symptoms online and listen to other people who do not believe in divine health and healing. By doing this, they nearly extinguish their faith, which is the only hope anyone has.

If thoughts about dying begin to enter your mind, just entertain them for a while, and I can assure you they will multiply. Keep meditating on those thoughts from the enemy and you will not be able to sleep at night or even feel like getting out of bed the next morning.

How many precious, blood-washed people, when they feel a symptom coming on, the first thing they begin to confess is, "I have it." Then they boldly confess what the doctor told them is going to happen next, or what a cousin-in-law said they had seen happen to people in their experience. They have affectively bypassed their faith with their words and called sickness and disease into their life.

In ignorance of their words' harmful effects, people begin to say, "I have this sickness," or, "I have this pain." "I have this difficulty that is getting worse all the time." So faith begins to decrease and the stealing of a healing is well under way.

Resisting at the Onset

What you need to do is resist the enemy at the onset of doubt or fear. When your body feels sick, call it healed. You're not saved because of how you feel. You're saved because of what Jesus accomplished on the cross through the Atonement. When you receive an evil report, reject it and resist the enemy, and boldly declare, "I WILL BELIEVE THE REPORT OF THE LORD." His report says that I am healed, blessed, delivered, and set free from all sickness and disease.

Always remember, there is nothing bad that can ever happen in your life but what Jesus can do something good about it. To keep the enemy from stealing your healing, at the onset of any attack of the enemy, *speak just the opposite of whatever the devil is lying to you about and trying to do.*

I know a mighty pastor whose wife was attacked by cancer. She was not given a good report by the doctors. When she talked to her husband, he asked her, "What were the first words that you spoke when you heard the bad report?" The woman of God told her husband, "I immediately said, 'I shall live and not die and will declare the works of the Lord.'"

That was many, many years ago, and today, this mighty woman of God is the very picture of health. God blessed her with healing and a long, healthy life. With her husband, together they are touching untold thousands of people for God and eternity.

The words of faith that you speak will cause you to live and not die. It also keeps the enemy from ever being able to steal your healing

3

When Healing Comes

Did you know that sometimes healing is a process and sometimes it's instantaneous? But healing always comes.

Then Jesus said to the Roman officer, "Go back home. Because you believed, it has happened." And the young servant was healed that same hour. (Matthew 8:13 NLT)

When healing comes, invite it to stay. Don't ever send healing packing with words of doubt and unbelief. A lying symptom may return; fear may ask to spend the night. But don't ever let healing go.

Healing is precious. Healing is obtained by faith, and it is retained by faith. Never let go of the manifestation of God's healing power.

The Process of Manifested Healing

Brother Kenneth Hagin tells the story of being raised up off a bed of affliction reading Grandma's Methodist Bible. Through a process of time—as I recall around 18 months to 2 years—God totally healed his deformed heart.

After being bedridden for years, he was about 6 feet tall and weighed only about 120 pounds. He looked like death warmed over, and when he went back to school, just the sight of him scared the teachers and students.

His kind-hearted principal called him into the office one day to ask him if he should even be at school. They were afraid he was actually going to drop dead. Brother Hagin, as a teenage boy, said to the principal, "I'm standing on the Word. I believe I'm healed."

The principal's heart was touched when he saw his faith. The principal then told him, "If that is what you are believing, then you can stay at school, but anytime you need to leave the class, just get up and leave."

Did you know that the devil would come

and torment young Brother Hagin's mind and tell him to leave class? These were demonic suggestions. But Brother Hagin stayed. He stayed in class and he stayed in faith.

If he had lost his faith, he would have lost his healing. And if he had lost his healing, he would have lost his life. *What you do with the Word and ignoring demonic suggestions has everything to do with keeping your healing.*

Decades later, Brother Hagin told about waking up in the night with some of the most alarming heart symptoms. The same symptoms he had years ago as a boy. Once again, the enemy was trying to steal his healing. But Brother Hagin prayed quietly, and this Scripture came to him:

And being not weak in faith, he considered

not his own body now dead, when he was about an hundred years old, neither yet the deadness of Sarah's womb. (Romans 4:19)

So Brother Hagin just went to sleep in faith. The enemy could not steal what God had done for him. Brother Hagin lived well into his 80s and touched millions with the wonderful Gospel of Good News.

Remember friend, what God has done for one, He will do for others. It is because of God's great love that you are reading this book. The Word teaches us in Romans 2:11 that God is no respecter of persons, meaning He shows no partiality. In the Amplified Classic translation, it says:

For God shows no partiality [undue favor or

unfairness; with Him one man is not different from another].

Has God healed someone? Then He will heal you. Has God blessed someone? Then He will bless you. Receive it by faith, and never let it go.

The Consequences of Our Words

I know a story of a woman who was gloriously healed of total deafness in a tent meeting. My friend who is a great man of God had been preaching the Good News of the Lord Jesus Christ. This woman who had been deaf all her life was healed by the power of God and received a wonderful miracle.

After most everyone had left the meeting, the preacher heard this awful commotion in the back. A man said, "My mother has locked herself in the car and is screaming. She won't let anyone else in."

Someone asked the son, "What happened to the precious woman?" and they found out that on the way to the car, the mother—who had been so gloriously healed—said to her son, "I hope it lasts." Immediately, she was deaf again. It was the stealing of a healing by the enemy.

The precious lady's fear-based words of doubt and unbelief opened a door for the devil to walk through. It is so important to say words of faith, before we are healed, and after we are healed.

Faith-filled words open the way for God to

move, and faith-filled words keep the enemy from being able to make us sick. You and I are speaking spirits that live in a body, and everything that we believe and speak creates our circumstances.

The Bible teaches that every one of us will stand before God someday (Hebrews 9:27). At The Judgment, every one of us will give an account of every idle word that is spoken. Yes, every single word.

> But I say unto you, That every idle word that men shall speak, they shall give account thereof in the day of judgment. (Matthew 12:36)

Trust me, I've learned when I have missed it with my words to say, "I cancel those words in the Name of Jesus." Our words have tremendous consequences and power attached to them. That is why the Word says in Proverbs 18:21:

"Death and life are in the power of the tongue."

What you say will either bring healing into your body or push healing away. It can cause you, or even someone else that you love, to be sick if they believe your words of unbelief.

4

Jesus Is Willing

Jesus, our Lord and Savior, has already spoken about your healing, and His forever answer is, "I WILL."

In one of the villages, Jesus met a man with an advanced case of leprosy. When the man saw Jesus, he bowed with his face to the ground, begging to be healed. "Lord," he said, "if you are willing, you can heal me and make me clean." Jesus reached out and touched him. "I am willing," he said. "Be healed!" And instantly the leprosy disappeared. (Luke 5:12-13 NLT)

The Word of God that you believe and speak is the Word that will work for you. Even your own words that you speak that are based on God's Word will set you free and keep you free. When you speak words of faith, it is as powerful as Jesus walking into your room and speaking wonderful words of life to you.

Jesus spoke to the fig tree (Matthew 21:19); He spoke to the storm on the Sea of Galilee (Matthew 8:26); Jesus spoke the word for the Roman Centurion's servant, and his servant was healed (Matthew 8:13); And when satan came to tempt Jesus, immediately Jesus said, "*It is written...*" (Matthew 4:4).

You can do the same thing Jesus did when the enemy tries to come against you in your thought life. You can drive the devil away just like Jesus did by quoting the Word of God.

The Blessings of a Bold Confession

Oh, how often in the early days of my ministry I was with people that talked trouble for hours. Then they ended it with, "Well, I guess all we can do about it is pray." You can do a lot more than that. Quit talking trouble and problems, and speak just the opposite of what the enemy is trying to do in your life.

You don't have to talk God into doing what

He has already said in *His* Word that He will do. Now, that will cut out most of the conversation that a lot of people—and even some preachers—have.

Miracles are instant, and healing is a process, but oftentimes a very quick process. What you say or don't say can speed things up or slow things down. Again, you don't have to talk God into anything that He has already written and promised in His Word. So never again doubt, and start simply saying the promises of God.

A blind squirrel can get an acorn once in a while, but do you want to launch your faith to a whole new atmosphere? Start speaking the Word every day over your life, over those that you love, and over circumstances in your and your family's lives. Boldly confess the promises of God.

See, if you shopped online, after stepping away from the computer, you would boldly confess, "I just ordered this and it is coming any day now!" Then you would begin to look for it.

Jesus has done all that He is going to do about your salvation and about your healing. All that is left is for you to believe and receive and keep praising God.

Friend, it is time for you to speak. It is time for you to speak as if Jesus, our Lord and Savior, has come into your room and said, "Whatsoever you say, I will do." (Mark 11:24)

Is there a mountain in your life? I want to encourage you to quit speaking about the mountain and start speaking to the mountain.

Truly I tell you, whoever says to this mountain, Be lifted up and thrown into the sea!

and does not doubt at all in his heart but believes that what he says will take place, it will be done for him. (Mark 11:23 AMPC)

It is vital that you start speaking what you want God to do, and absolutely refuse to speak about what the devil has done or is trying to do in your life and family.

There will surely come a day when you want to give a victorious testimony and talk about how the enemy was defeated, but talking about the enemy under those circumstances brings strength to you, not doubt and fear.

If you'll quit talking trouble, and start talking faith, it will transform your life forever. Constantly be thanking and praising God for what He has done and is going to do.

You resist the enemy with your mind, and

you resist the enemy by speaking the Word of God—especially the Word of God that Jesus gives to you in the hour of need. Say this confession:

I win every time. I always come out on top. God is for me, who can be against me? I am walking in a good path. My mind is sound and my body is healthy. I walk in peace and prosperity. No strategy, now or ever, will defeat me. I am blessed. I have on the full armor of God. I fight the good fight of faith, and I win every time.

Say it every day, and never give your faith a day off—Never!

5

The Expectation of Faith

In your city or hometown, there is probably a good old boy whose reputation and name are a reflection of his bad deeds. The infamy of the outlaw grows and grows as the years go by because of the bad life that has been lived.

The Bible is a book of God's exploits (what God has done), combined with precious promises of what He will do when we have faith. What Jesus has done and what He wants to do should be preached all over the earth.

The preached Word causes the Lord's Name to be lifted high and faith to rise in people's hearts; it causes people's expectation to rise, so they don't dwell on their situations but instead on the promises of Scripture.

You may have a situation or problem arise, and if you dwell on the problem, even more trouble will come. But when you find the answers in Scripture, and claim them by meditating on and speaking them, something good happens: As expectation and Bible faith arise, *healings* and *miracles* begin to take place.

Sadly, though, a lot of God's precious children don't know how to do this because they have never sat under *anointed preaching*.

Believers have to be taught something to believe and stand on.

God's Word Must Be Taught

The Word of God is the standard for our faith. *The Word causes faith to rise in our spirit-man, and it is absolutely life-changing—for now and for eternity.* If you have never been taught how to believe, meditate on, and speak God's mighty Word, you are at such a disadvantage in lifting up the shield of faith.

But oh, I have such good news for you: You can learn to believe and learn to exercise your faith. Trust me, I know. When I learned, by God's grace, to do what I've just taught you, it changed my life forever. It changed my entire family's lives forever.

God's Name has not been exalted like it should be because the Word has not been preached in our pulpits like it should be. There are churches where you will never be healed there and never be blessed because the Word is not preached there.

A steady diet of the lies that "God made you sick," "Healing is not for everyone," and "We will understand it better by and by..." aren't going to get you healed or help you stay healed.

Oh, the precious times, again and again, that the Holy Spirit has quickened a verse to me and my whole life and ministry were forever changed. How often, under the anointed teaching and preaching of the Word, I have received a life-changing, forever Word from God. That's why it's so vital to be in a church that has faith and teaches the Word—and vital that you be supernaturally connected to people of faith that believe the *Word of God.*

Do your friends have faith? Do they speak expectantly of the *promises of God* coming to pass in their life and in yours? Is there an atmosphere of faith at your church that God can do anything? The Word that you sit under every week has a big impact on your ability to believe and to receive.

All of the glorious tomorrows God has planned for you are wrapped up in the Holy Spirit quickening a Word from God to you and in you believing and confessing that Word of the Lord.

It is truly amazing the deception of the American church that they think they can go to church for an hour a week and that is enough. It is not enough. Every day you must feed your spirit the promises of the Word on healing, confess them, and stand upon them, and you will begin to see your body line up with the Word.

Being Offended by the Word

The convicting power of the Holy Spirit is to be cherished and sought after. I know what it is to be in a church where a strong word from God's Word was being preached and it made me uncomfortable. It stretched me, convicted me, and knocked the unbelief out of me.

Years ago, I was pastoring a poor, little church in the inner city that was mainly made up of a group of homeless people that nobody else wanted. Often, on Thursday nights I would attend a megachurch, and I could barely afford the toll money on the Garden State Parkway to get there.

We were struggling and sometimes not even getting a salary. Our church battled to even keep the lights on in the ministry. So, poor me (literally) goes to this church that is telling me that it is not God's will for me to lack and go without. They were preaching that God wanted to prosper me, and how it was up to me to believe the Word, to build up my faith, to change my mindset, and to sow financial seed.

Believe me, I had to deal with being offended and wondering how on earth they were so blessed while I was so broke. They taught me about giving and confessing the Word, and I had a choice to make: I could receive the Word, or I could keep blaming the devil and take no personal responsibility for the predicament I was in.

I'm *so glad* that I chose to receive and believe the Word and not walk away offended. When the Holy Spirit convicts you of something in your life, or of a mindset that needs to change, it is because God loves you so much. *The decision to be loved by the convicting power of the Holy Spirit is allowing God to help you always stay on the right path.*

The decision to go with God's Word and not my feelings is one of the greatest decisions, by God's grace, that I ever have made. That decision changed my whole world and the world of my entire family and descendants.

Today, I am blessed beyond measure, and our ministry is growing by leaps and bounds, above and beyond all that I could ask or think. I have divine connections with Godly pastors and am privileged to preach in some of the most outstanding and precious churches in

America. God is opening doors for us that, driving on that Garden State Parkway years ago, I never could have dreamed possible in my wildest imagination. I'm so glad I didn't get offended over the preached Word and let the devil steal the wonderful life God had and has for me and my precious family.

When the Word came into our lives, faith came along with it. That faith allowed our family to be a part of founding Jericho Road Homeless Shelters at the church I pastored. That church is now thriving, and I believe that Jericho Road Homeless Shelters is well on its way to being a national ministry. Multiplied thousands of homeless people have been rescued from death and poverty. It is just the beginning. The work of God is growing in ways I never even dreamed, under the leadership of my son, Benjamin Dunfee.

Oh, the times the stinkin' devil came and lied to me, telling me that God's Word wouldn't and couldn't work for me, and that I was a victim. But something happened, and it changed my world forever; faith came.

By God's grace I believed, received, and started speaking the Word that I had been exposed to by hearing it. A spirit of faith came mightily upon me and I began to operate in the gift of faith. And that has made all the difference.

God has had us step into the overflow of *the supernatural.* I will thank and praise God all my life until Jesus comes back that I wasn't offended by the Word and instead *received it.*

Some people say, "Well, I went to church and got a touch." God wants to give you more than a touch. God wants to give you a complete transformation—body, soul, and spirit.

The devil's Biggest Fear

The enemy wants nothing more than to make you just as poor, wretched, sick, and unhappy as he can, so that you barely exist on the planet earth and live in total misery. The stupid devil wants to do everything he can to hinder you in every area of life. He wants to steal your money, take your health, and rob you of your joy. That's why he hates Bibles and hates preachers.

The devil's biggest fear is that you will hear the Word and that you will believe it. So when you do believe the Word, the enemy will come and try to steal it from you immediately.

When they hear, Satan comes at once and [by force] takes away the message which is sown in them. (Mark 4:15 AMPC)

But you don't have to let him do it. Don't allow yourself, your family, and future generations to be robbed of the blessings of God. Renew your mind with the Word of God every day. Believe and confess that the promises of God are for you. The Holy Spirit will put such an *anointed expectation* in your spirit that every morning you will get up expecting to receive.

6

Why Do You Believe What You Believe?

We don't get our doctrine (which is what we believe) from other people's experiences. *The Word of God is to be the foundation for all our doctrine.*

The Bible is the Good News message of the good things that God has in store for us. Good

47

things in this lifetime and for all of eternity.

Every one of us must make a personal decision as to whether or not we are going to believe or doubt God's Word. By *faith* I choose to believe and I choose to receive *God's best* because that's what the Bible teaches. This decision is whether or not to receive the promises of God for you and your family.

I have met many born-again and even spirit-filled people who didn't believe in—and even wanted to fight about—prosperity and healing. Had I listened to them, I wouldn't have the money that I need to touch tens of thousands, and soon, I believe, millions of souls.

But Christ has rescued us from the curse pronounced by the law. When he was hung on the cross, he took upon himself the curse

48

for our wrongdoing. For it is written in the Scriptures, "Cursed is everyone who is hung on a tree." Through Christ Jesus, God has blessed the Gentiles with the same blessing he promised to Abraham, so that we who are believers might receive the promised Holy Spirit through faith. (Galatians 3:13-14 NLT)

The blessing of the Lord—it makes [truly] rich, and He adds no sorrow with it [neither does toiling increase it]. (Proverbs 10:22 AMPC)

I could have listened to some people and been talked out of my healing and *blessing*. Oh, the excellent, tailor-made opportunities I have had to get bitter, quit, and feel sorry for myself. But by God's *great grace* I never gave up. Jesus and my wife, Debbie, just wouldn't let me.

God's Mercy is For You

At other times, I had this vague sense that I had missed it somewhere. It is almost always true when you do not have God's *perfect peace*.

We never have to put up with that in our lives for even a minute. Always make sure that what you believe is based upon the Scriptures and not upon what you feel or other people's traditions. Remember, any time that you don't have peace, it is usually a sign that you have missed it somewhere. God's Word promises peace to us.

And the peace of God, which transcends all

understanding, will guard your hearts and your minds in Christ Jesus. (Philippians 4:7 NIV)

My precious friend, does this describe you today? Are you struggling beneath a heavy load? Is the little devil trying to steal something from you? Even today, you may sense that something is missing in your life and ministry. I have glorious good news for you: The Lord loves to help people who have missed it in any area.

Let the Holy Spirit show you in His Word where you went off-track. God's mercies are new every morning and Jesus stands with arms open wide, ready to heal you, restore you, and give you back double for your trouble. Every-thing—and I mean everything—that the enemy has stolen from you is going to be *totally restored*.

Get it settled in your heart that God is a good God. Get it settled in your spirit that God wants to bless you exceedingly, abundantly, above and beyond all that you can ask or think. In the Amplified Classic translation, Ephesians 3:20 says:

"Now to Him Who, by (in consequence of) the [action of His] power that is at work within us, is able to [carry out His purpose and] do superabundantly, far over and above all that we [dare] ask or think [infinitely beyond our highest prayers, desires, thoughts, hopes, or dreams]."

Simply put: God's plan for our lives is a lot bigger and better than our plans! God thinks bigger than we do and His plan is a perfect plan. A plan that is complete and is designed to help us fulfill our destiny. A destiny which was planned for us from the foundation of the world.

His plan is larger and better, and *His plan* includes *total healing* for our bodies. It also includes supernatural blessing in our finances. God's plan for our future is a wonderful life of purposeful living here on earth. Then we spend all of eternity in Heaven with Jesus, our loved ones and our friends. It is far-reaching and more excellent in scope and influence than our little man-made, man-inspired plans.

Have your plans failed? Has the enemy stolen from you something precious that God gave you? I have good news for you: The devil has to give it back, and he has to give back more than he took. Ask God for big things. Ask largely.

And ask joyfully in faith, believing that when you ask, you receive.

7

Conquering Unbelief

So we see that they could not enter in because of unbelief. (Hebrews 3:19)

Unbelief is a spirit. In fact, the whole
Israelite nation got a spirit of doubt and
unbelief on them because of the words of just a
few carnal people. *A whole nation* was held at

bay and kept from going into the Promised Land all because of unbelief.

What kind of spirit is the overriding spirit that you live your life by? What kind of spirit are you passing onto your family?

Unbelief (especially spoken unbelief) opens the door for the enemy to bring many sicknesses and diseases upon you. Words of doubt and unbelief short-circuit the power of God. There is such power in our words that they bring death and life (Proverbs 18:21).

The way that you lay claim to the promises of God is by speaking *words of faith*. Your words of faith will shut the door on the enemy's ability to take away your future by taking away your health. Faith words slam the door in the devil's face every time.

Some things should never, ever be spoken

by us or over the people we love. All of the unkind, doubtful, or even evil things that have been spoken over you can *all* be canceled through the blood of Jesus.

In Jesus' mighty Name, say: *"I cancel the bad words that have been spoken over my life. They shall not come to pass. My whole family and I walk in the blessing of God. The angels of the Lord surround us, and our house is built upon the solid Rock, Jesus Christ. My family and I have a bright future and will have long, blessed, healthy lives. We will fulfill our God-given destinies. We will do the will of God. And we are blessed to be a blessing."*

The Watered-Down Word

Your spirit was designed to be filled with faith; and faith comes from the Word of God. If you went outside and put sand in your gas tank, your car would not operate very well, would it? Your car also will not operate very well if you water down the fuel that you put in it.

What if you said, "Mark, I think I will water down my gas with 10% water. Think of the savings"? That's one way to look at it. But your car wouldn't go far before it would break down.

There are lots of fine, Christian people that have had a ton of financial, spiritual, and physical breakdowns, and it's because the Word has been watered down where they go to church. Their church has no faith. No Victory. *What you sit under, you will become.*

By reading the Word of God and following God's peace, you can easily tell what is going on in your life.

Go all the way, right now, by putting your total trust and complete faith in Jesus. *And then immediately begin to speak what you desire God to do for you.* Find a Scripture that pertains to your promise, and start meditating on it, and speaking it in *Jesus' mighty, wonderful Name.*

Meet the enemy head-on with your Word weapon:

> Put on salvation as your helmet, and take the sword of the Spirit, which is the word of God. (Ephesians 6:17 NLT)

For hundreds of years, Christians had no Bible. But they did have testimonies of their own and of others, and they repeated and rehearsed them, again and again, by telling all who listened. They overcame by pleading the blood *and constantly telling their testimony of the great things God had done for them.*

"The good fight of faith" (1 Timothy 6:12) is to see yourself healed and whole, and always staying that way. See yourself healed and well until Jesus comes back, and always testify that you are healed.

Has the enemy tried to steal your healing? Did your healing start to manifest, but now symptoms have reappeared? Now is *definitely not the time* to talk to doubtful people who do not believe in *divine healing*.

People who meditate on and constantly speak unbelief—this is the kind of thing they say: "Now, we don't know why God did this to you…" But it is not God who made you sick. It is the stinkin' devil who's doing it!

Bad things are from the enemy, and you

can bind them. Good things come from God, and you can loose them. Why don't you bind what the enemy is trying to pull in your life, and loose what Heaven is trying to do in your life?

> Whatever you bind on earth will be bound in heaven, and whatever you loose on earth will be loosed in heaven. (Matthew 18:18 NKJV)

Constantly praise God for health, strength, long life, and peace. Talk health and healing. Constantly confess, "I walk in strength and divine health." *Your future and whole family's future depends upon what you think about and what you say.*

The Role of a Renewed Mind

If you exercise doubt and fear, and if you keep looking for symptoms, symptoms will come. If you are moved by feelings instead of faith in the Word and acting upon the Word, you can struggle every day. The Word is not based upon how I feel but is based upon God's Name; and God can never lie.

> For those who live according to the flesh set their minds on the things of the flesh, but those who live according to the Spirit, the things of the Spirit. For to be carnally minded is death, but to be spiritually minded is life and peace. (Romans 8:5-6 NKJV)

In New England, where I come from, the old country farmhouses have a front door and a back door. Especially in old times, if people liked you, they'd invite you in to sit down at their table while they feed you and commune with you. They might even sit in a rocking chair with you on their front porch and spend an enjoyable hour or two visiting and telling stories. *But if they didn't like you*, then you might get pushed out the back door or never even let in the front door. *Some thoughts should absolutely never be let past the front steps of our minds.*

Casting down imaginations, and every high thing that exalteth itself against the knowledge of God, and bringing into captivity every thought to the obedience of Christ. (2 Corinthians 10:5)

2 Corinthians 10:5 says we are to take every thought captive! We all have to be watchful about entertaining every thought that just pops into our minds. Some thoughts come from the enemy and other thoughts just come from our fleshly mind. One thing is for sure, if it doesn't line up with the Word, just push it out of your head.

> Instead, let the Spirit renew your thoughts and attitudes. Put on your new nature, created to be like God—truly righteous and holy. (Ephesians 4:23-24 NLT)

You must learn to renew your mind on a daily basis. Renewing your mind doesn't just fall on you like pouring rain falls down on your head when you have no umbrella.

Renewing your mind is also not something you do all at once, for all time. You have to renew the way you think on a daily basis and constantly reinforce the decision to think right by faith.

Renewing your mind is a process and is done by taking your thoughts captive by faith. We *all* have to train our minds to think on whatever is *true, honest, just, pure, lovely, and of a good report,* according to Philippians 4:8. It really means to *fix your mind* on these things.

When a thought that isn't good comes, replace it with a thought based on the Word. Meditate on the Word. The truth will set you free! (John 8:32).

In fact, speak out something from the Word of God that is just the opposite of the stinkin' lie that the enemy is trying to get you to believe.

Ask Jesus to help you totally renew your mind by the *power of the Holy Ghost*. When it happens, a description of your belief system and personality becomes the *fruit of the Spirit*.

> But the Holy Spirit produces this kind of fruit in our lives: love, joy, peace, patience, kindness, goodness, faithfulness, gentleness, and self-control. There is no law against these things! (Galatians 5:22-23 NLT)

8

Lifting up the Shield of Faith

The Bible says that Abraham received a glorious promise that he and his wife Sarah would have a son (Genesis 15:4). But it also says Abraham considered not his own body.

And not being weak in faith, he did not

consider his own body, already dead (since he was about a hundred years old), and the deadness of Sarah's womb. (Romans 4:19 NKJV)

If Abraham had looked at himself in the mirror, he might not have liked what he saw. There was no way in the natural that he could have a child.

Friend, if you go by how you feel and by what you see, you will miss it. Go by what the Word says. Stay with the Word!

You'll have to reach out daily in faith for the supernatural—supernatural favor, blessing, health, and finances. When the enemy tries to come against your mind, in Jesus' Name do this:

Hold up the shield of faith to stop the fiery arrows of the devil. (Ephesians 6:16 NLT)

Every day we need to lift up the shield of faith.

Robbed of the Blessings of Life

The devil will take as much room in your life as you allow him to take. Just as much territory in your life as you are willing to concede through doubt and unbelief. The devil is more than willing to steal and destroy. That's why you need to be strong in the Lord and in the power of His might! (Ephesians 6:10)

How many precious people have been robbed of the blessings of life? Blessings given to them by Jesus. Their blessings stolen away because they allowed the enemy back into their thought life. Simply, they did not resist the enemy and stand firm in the faith.

> Leave no [such] room or foothold for the devil [give no opportunity to him]. (Ephesians 4:27 AMPC)

Jesus had the enemy come to him on the Mount of Temptation. Jesus did not say, "Don't you know who I am?" Or, "I'm so tired and wish I could have a break." No, Jesus quoted the Word of God. And when He spoke the Word of God, the devil then departed from Him for a season.

God's Word puts the devil on the run and keeps him on the run. Resisting the enemy with your words continuously keeps the enemy out of your life.

Jesus said that in this world you're going to have tribulation—but fear not, for I have overcome the world.

> I have told you these things, so that in Me you may have [perfect] peace and confidence. In the world you have tribulation and trials and distress and frustration; but be of good cheer [take courage; be confident, certain, undaunted]! For I have overcome the world. [I have deprived it of power to harm you and have conquered it for you.] (John 16:33 AMPC)

As long as you live in this body and live on this planet, you will have to stand in faith and resist the enemy of your faith. But I have some good news for you!

He Who lives in you is greater (mightier) than he who is in the world. (1 John 4:4 AMPC)

The Greater One resides within you and is so willing and able to guide and *supernaturally bless* you in every decision you have to make. The Greater One is on your side, and you can lean on Him. I sure know that I do each and every day. Jesus, the Greater One, wants you to win every day, every time!

There is no—absolutely no—substitute for faith. None. And there is no substitute for withstanding the enemy by speaking the Word of Almighty God.

The devil Wants You Miserable

Imagine if you heard a sound at night, looked outside, and someone had broken into your garage and was trying to steal your rake. Here's what most of you would do: Run outside in your pajamas and wrestle with them on the front lawn.

You would pull out a shotgun and say, "Now, do you want me to pull this trigger, or are you going to get off my property?" You'd call the cops. You'd scream at the thief, "You are not going to have my rake! It belongs to me and you can't have it!"

While waiting for the police, you'd holler, "THIEF! THIEF!" at the top of your lungs. If you woke up all the neighbors who have to get up at 5:00 AM, so be it, because nobody is getting your stuff.

Yet, when the devil tries to steal health and money from God's people, silent submission is the order of the day for most Christians. Either silence or they talk to other church members and they all wonder why God has done this to them. It is not Jesus. It is the devil! Anything bad that is happening or trying to happen in your life is not God. It is the enemy.

So many people protect their garden rakes more than they do their health, money, and peace of mind. They sit and watch and say, "Well, what can anyone do?" Then add, "We will understand it better by and by." No, I understand it right now! The devil is trying to make your life miserable and steal everything that you've got!

The enemy will try to get you to see yourself busted and disgusted, sick, poor, wretched and weary. He'll try to get you to talk about it and speak words of doubt and fear, which actually increases and opens up doors for the enemy to attack further. That is not God's will for any of His children.

The enemy will plant a thought in your mind that is wrong, usually in your imagination. Then he will try to get you to meditate on that distorted thought. Then the stupid devil will try to get you to speak fearful words about what you were just thinking concerning some sickness or being defeated. Then here comes the manifestation, along with demonic taunting and lying thoughts that say, "I told you so," or, "You were never really healed." If you live by just what you see and hear and feel, it will cause you to always be under attack.

Friend, we are people of the Spirit, and because of that, we are called to walk in the Spirit. *You are a spirit that lives in a body*. Added to that, as people of faith, we resist the enemy by speaking the Word of Almighty God.

Always speak just the opposite of anything that the enemy lies to you about. If the devil ever tells you that you can never be healed, turn the *Word of God* loose on the enemy.

If the enemy tells you that you will always be broke, say, "I am the blessed of the Lord." Remind the little devil that the Lord is your shepherd and that you do not—and never will—want for anything.

When the devil leaves you a mental news report from Hell that you have this or that tribulation to look forward to, simply say, "IT IS WRITTEN," just like *Jesus* did. Here is exactly

what will happen next: The little devil will have
to flee.

> Resist the devil [stand firm against him], and
> he will flee from you. (James 4:7 AMPC)

9

It's Your Time

Have you ever had something stolen by the devil and then sought help in prayer from some unbelieving-believer? They act real pious as they religiously lift their face and squint, praying, "If it be thy will, oh God, do something about this situation."

Friend, you don't have to pray "If it be thy

will, oh God" when God's will is plainly stated in God's Word. God's Word is His will.

God loves us so much that He gave us a book. Have you ever heard someone say, "Well, you never know what the Lord will do"? I know what God will do because in God's Word, it plainly says what God will do! All we have to do is receive it by faith.

The Promises of God

For all the promises of God in Him are Yes, and in Him Amen, to the glory of God through us. (2 Corinthians 1:20 NKJV)

When you have received the promise of healing, never let the devil talk you out of it. *Never let the devil steal what God has given you.* You don't have to ever again let the devil steal from you what God wants to do or has already done.

There are no expiration dates on the promises of God. *Everyone who believes receives.* Everyone who exercises their faith and follows the Word of God gets the same response. The promises of God are "Yes" and "Amen." God says yes, *so now we simply say yes to His promises!*

Please do not say no to something God has said yes to! Receive and *keep* the overwhelming *goodness* of God and His *promises* written in His Word! God is the God of the "YES!"

I do not preach "Lottery Jesus" across America and around the world. We do not preach "Lucky Number Jesus," which is basically saying, "You might get lucky if your number is picked in Heaven." You will never hear us preach, "God might help you if He is in the right mood."

We boldly proclaim the truth about Jesus, who was wounded for our transgressions and bruised for our iniquities, and by His stripes we were healed (Isaiah 53:5). We preach Jesus Christ, the same yesterday, today, and forever (Hebrews 13:8). We still cast out devils (Mark 16:17). We still lay hands on the sick and they recover (Mark 16:18). We preach the absolute goodness of God (John 10:10).

> But He was wounded for our transgressions, He was bruised for our guilt and iniquities; the chastisement [needful to obtain] peace and well-being for us was upon Him, and with the stripes [that wounded] Him we are healed and made whole. (Isaiah 53:5 AMPC)

We lay hands on the sick for precious people to receive *forever healing*—not healing for a moment, but for all time. Healing may come in a moment, but it will stay until the Lord comes or the Lord calls you to Heaven. (By the way, you don't have to be sick when you die. You can just fall asleep in the arms of Jesus.)

Don't ever let the devil steal your healing. Confess, "I'm well." Stand strong in faith, and don't ever listen to doubting people who speak words of death. Let Jesus bring covenant friends into your life, who once were sick but now are whole.

It's your time.

Your best days are ahead of you. It's time for you to see yourself prospering in your body, in your soul, and in your spirit.

It's time to step into the *promises of God*,

where everything you and your family touch is *blessed.*

Your *blessing* is dependent on what you *see* and on what you *say.* Struggling people tend to *see* themselves struggling in the future as much as they are struggling now. But faith will cause you to see something different *right now.*

Sick people often have a mental image of their health getting worse and continuing to go downhill as more time goes by. *But faith will cause you to see yourself well right now.*

When the enemy comes to steal what God has done for you, resist him! Go right back to the basics. Build your faith simply by finding a Scripture that the Holy Spirit reveals to you and *stand in faith on it.* Guard your confession and *stop speaking about how your symptoms feel. Speak what the Word says has already been accomplished on the cross in regards to your healing.*

Trusting What You Cannot Feel

God's Word is *truth based upon the character of God*. How you feel at the moment is not to be compared to the truth of God's Word.

Physical and emotional feelings change, sometimes on an hourly basis, but God's Word never changes. Feelings have nothing to do with whether or not God wants to heal you. In fact, God may have already healed you but it hasn't totally manifested yet.

If you confess how you feel at the moment, you can open a door for the enemy to steal your healing. *You can trust your faith, but you can't always trust your feelings.*

God is our Heavenly source that never fails or runs dry. I am not going to let a mood swing or how my flesh may feel about something rule my life. *Your future is to be guided by the Word of God and your faith in it.*

Enforce what the Word says about your circumstances. Don't put pressure on people or on yourself; put pressure on the Word. Stand on it and confess it every day until the Word manifests and completely changes your circumstances.

I don't regret a time that I have used my measure of faith and believed for what I could not see, feel, or hear in the natural. The Word has always worked and always will. The Word works every time!

Oh, the dear people who have been lied to and deceived into thinking that God doesn't want to do good things for them. It's just not true.

For too many Christians, "normal" is living defeated. Never settle for that in your life. God has not changed His mind about healing or about doing good things in your life.

Your Healing Moment

Have you missed it? Well, I have good news for you: The Word of God says,

> Goodness and mercy shall follow me all the days of my life: and I will dwell in the house of the Lord for ever. (Psalm 23:6)

The enemy will steal what you allow him

to steal. He's so willing to lie to you each and every day if you are willing to listen.

Be strong in the Lord, and in the power of his might. (Ephesians 6:10)

You have to get fed up with what the enemy has done and is trying to do in your life. Don't let the enemy steal your healing and the good life God has for you.

Even right now, let this be your faith moment of *total recovery*. A forever-healing moment. A healing from Jesus that your faith will never, ever release.

You will joyfully never be the same again as you walk in health, all of your life and for all eternity. What Jesus has done for one, He will do for you. Tell the good news to as many people as you can.

Today—and even *right now*—have a healing encounter with Jesus Christ, and never, ever let the devil talk you into losing it. You have a *healing* that is precious, and you will never let fear or doubt steal it away.

> For though we live in the world, we do not wage war as the world does. The weapons we fight with are not the weapons of the world. On the contrary, they have divine power to demolish strongholds. We demolish arguments and every pretension that sets itself up against the knowledge of God, and we take captive every thought to make it obedient to Christ. (2 Corinthians 10:3-5 NIV)

Pray this prayer for healing of any kind:

Heavenly Father, in Jesus' Name, I receive Your healing, which was paid for with the stripes of the whip on Jesus' back. You said these signs shall follow them that believe: They shall lay hands on the sick and they shall recover. I receive my healing now by faith in the Lord Jesus Christ. It is not because of my goodness but by faith that I receive divine healing in my body. A healing from Heaven because of Jesus. A healing that I will never lose. I speak that from this second on, I will recover. By faith, I receive being made whole. From this moment on, I will speak health and not sickness. I am forever healed, and I will be a testimony of God's healing and grace. In Jesus' mighty Name, amen.

Evangelist Reinhard Bonnke told me once, "*If every person in every wheelchair got healed and then went to Hell, what would it really matter that they got healed?*" Pray today this prayer of *salvation* in simple faith. Believe every word that you pray, and meet me in Heaven one day because of *Jesus Christ,* who died on the cross for all of our sins:

Heavenly Father, in Jesus' Name, please forgive me for all of my sins. I believe that Jesus is the true Son of God, and I claim Jesus' shed blood on the cross of Calvary to pay for my sins. Wash me clean from all of my sins, and I will serve You for the rest of my life. One day, I want to go to Heaven and live with You forever.

Made in the USA
Middletown, DE
10 August 2020

14736329R00060